NINJA
Princess
DETECTIVES

PALACE
PUZZLER

by Kyla Steinkraus

Illustrated by Katie Wood

Rourke
Educational Media
rourkeeducationalmedia.com

a division of
Carson
Dellosa
Education

www.rourkeeducationalmedia.com

Edited by: *Kim Thompson*

Cover layout by: *Rhea Magaro-Wallace*

Interior layout by: *Kathy Walsh*

Cover and interior illustrations by: *Katie Wood*

Library of Congress PCN Data

Palace Puzzler / Kyla Steinkraus
(Ava and Gabby Danger: Ninja Princess Detectives)
ISBN 978-1-73161-484-1 (hard cover) (alk. paper)
ISBN 978-1-73161-291-5 (soft cover)
ISBN 978-1-73161-589-3 (e-Book)
ISBN 978-1-73161-694-4 (ePub)

Library of Congress Control Number: 2019932386

Printed in the United States of America,
North Mankato, Minnesota

Dear Guardian/Educator,

Introduce your child to the wonderful world of reading with our leveled readers. Your growing reader will be continuously engaged as he or she is guided from one level to the next. Each level is carefully built to provide your child with the reading skills and knowledge to be a confident reader! Ultimately, we want your child to develop a love of reading.

Level 1 *Learning to Read*
High frequency words, basic sentences, large type, labels, full color illustrations to help young readers better comprehend the text

Level 2 *Beginning to Read Alone*
Short sentences, familiar words, simple plot, easy-to-read fonts

Level 3 *Reading on Your Own*
Short paragraphs, easy-to-follow plots, vocabulary is increasingly challenging, exciting stories

Level 4 *Proficient Reader*
Chapters, engaging stories, challenging vocabulary, multiple text features

Reading should be a pleasurable experience. A child who enjoys reading reads more, and a child who reads more becomes a better reader. Your child will grow with exposure to broad vocabulary and literary techniques, and will develop deeper critical thinking and comprehension skills. We are excited to be a part of your child's reading journey.

Happy reading,
Rourke Educational Media

Table of Contents

Chapter One

Don't Be Angry

"I have a surprise for you, Sensei Suki," Ava Danger said as she hid something behind her back.

"You'll never guess what it is," her sister, Gabby, said.

"I can guess," offered their friend Alex.

"Shh," Jade said.

Sensei Suki smiled at them. "I never say no to a surprise."

Ava walked across the squishy mats in the

royal training room toward her martial arts teacher.

The class was practicing at the palace instead of at the ninja school this morning. Workers were busy transforming the school for the annual Taekwondo Tournament of Champions. It was only one day away!

"I made it myself," Ava said proudly as she held out her gift. She'd worked all day in the palace kitchen. She hadn't even tasted a bit of the cookie dough. She saved it all for Sensei Suki.

Sensei Suki carefully unwrapped a giant, gooey cookie. "A triple chocolate brownie cookie! My favorite!"

"Happy birthday!" Gabby and Ava sang together.

Sensei Suki's eyes widened in surprise. "How did you know?"

"A good ninja always knows," Gabby said with a wink. "It's the ninja way!"

Ava and Gabby were princesses and ninjas-in-training. They lived in the palace at the top of the hill with their parents, the king and queen of Klue.

Ava was older, with straight brown hair and glasses, while Gabby had short curly blonde hair that sprang up all over her head. They both loved dressing up in fancy gowns. They also loved working up a sweat practicing martial arts. They hoped to be as skilled as their mother and grandmother one day. The women still often performed secret missions for the kingdom.

But what Ava and Gabby really, truly loved most was a good mystery. In fact, they were known around Klue as the Ninja Princess Detectives. If anyone in the kingdom had a case to solve, they always came to Ava and Gabby Danger.

"Aren't you going to take a bite?" Ava asked as Sensei Suki started to wrap the cookie.

"Of course." Sensei Suki pressed her hand to her stomach before she took a small bite. "Mmmm," she mumbled around a mouthful of brownie cookie. "Delicious."

The class laughed.

"Keep practicing, guys." Sensei Suki leaned down and grabbed the bottle of ginger ale her husband brought her before the start of class. She twisted open the lid and took a long drink. "All of Klue will be watching tomorrow!"

While Sensei Suki was distracted with her soda and cookie, Mateo darted to the edge of the mat, stuck his hand in his rumpled backpack, and pulled out a handful of cheese crackers.

"What kind of cookie makes you rich?" Mateo asked. He was the class jokester. He paused only a second before he answered, "A fortune cookie!"

"Ha ha ha!" Erk croaked from Ava's uniform pocket.

"Shhh!" Ava whispered. "You're not supposed to be here."

Erk was their pet frog. Only the princesses could understand him. He taught them to speak Ribbit soon after he'd shown up at the palace. They sometimes wondered if he was a magical prince stuck in a frog body. But neither princess ever tried to kiss him to find out if it was one of those fairy tale spells. That was just too gross. Besides, they liked Erk just the way he was.

"You need to focus, Mateo," Alex said, "or you won't win a trophy."

Gabby watched as Alex rubbed his eyes. They were red and puffy.

"Are you okay, Alex?" she asked.

Alex nodded. "My new baby brother has been keeping me awake. It's been hard to practice, but I want to make my parents proud tomorrow."

Mateo stuffed cheese crackers in his mouth with a grin. "I know I can't beat Ava or Jade. I don't really care about winning."

"I care about winning," Jade said. She was good at everything, including martial arts. "In fact, I plan to win."

"So does Ava," Gabby said.

The whole class looked at Ava, waiting to see what she would say. Everyone knew she and Jade were the best martial artists in the kingdom.

Ava's cheeks grew hot. She really wanted to win too. But sometimes solving a mystery got in the way of practicing. "I'll do my best."

Mateo wiped his mouth with the back of his arm and left an orange smear across his face. "Let's see your best moves."

"Good idea," Sensei Suki said. She unzipped her zebra-print purse, tucked the wrapped, half-eaten cookie inside, and zipped it back up.

"I'll go first." Jade demonstrated her kicks. The class watched in awe as she spun, raised her knee, and leapt into a flying side kick.

Jade landed gracefully and demonstrated an axe kick, a hook kick, and a spinning back kick, all performed perfectly. She finished with a bow and grinned at Ava.

The triplets clapped their hands in excitement.

"Wow," Ella said.

"Double wow," Bella said.

"Triple wow!" Daniella said.

"Wonderful flying kick!" Sensei Suki sank down into her chair at the front of the room, her hand on her stomach. She looked a little pale. "Keep going! I'll watch from here."

It was Ava's turn. She spun and jumped and kicked. But her jump wasn't as high as Jade's. Her spin wasn't as fast. And when she landed, she almost lost her balance.

Ella and Bella gasped.

"It was a good try," Daniella said.

Ava's stomach sank. It didn't matter how hard she'd practiced. Jade was going to win the first-place trophy for sure.

"Looks like I'm better than you, after all," Jade bragged.

"That's not very nice," Gabby said, wrapping her arm around Ava's shoulders. But Ava shrugged her off.

"Don't be angry," Jade said smugly. "That's not good sportsmanship."

Ava wasn't angry—she was frustrated with herself. Before she could explain, Gabby grabbed her arm.

"Something's wrong with Sensei Suki!"

They all turned just in time to see Sensei Suki rush to the trash can, bend over, and throw up.

Chapter Two

Pukey Suki

Mr. Posh, the palace housekeeper, rushed into the training room. "Oh dear!"

"I'm okay." Sensei Suki tried to stand, then fell against Mr. Posh.

Mr. Posh put his arm around the sensei's shoulders. "You are certainly not okay!"

The class watched in stunned silence. Everyone looked worried.

"Will she be all right?" Ella asked.

"What about the tournament?" Jade asked.

Mr. Posh frowned. "Without Sensei Suki, there is no tournament."

Everyone gasped.

"My ... purse," Sensei Suki murmured as Mr. Posh helped her to the door.

"I've got it!" Alex dashed across the mats and grabbed the purse, then tripped and fell as he rushed back. He jumped to his feet, still holding the purse, his face wrinkled with worry and red with embarrassment. "Here you go, Sensei," he said quietly.

Before Sensei Suki could say thank you, Mr. Posh whisked her out of the room.

"Poor Sensei Suki," Gabby said. "What a terrible time to get sick."

"I hope she feels better soon," Alex said.

Mateo turned to Ava, frowning. "This is your fault."

Ava froze. "What?"

"You're the one who made the cookie," Mateo said. "She ate the cookie. She got sick. Isn't it obvious?"

"I smell foul play," Jade said.

"Why would Ava want to make Sensei Suki sick?" Gabby sputtered.

"If Ava can't win, then nobody can win." Jade put her hands on her hips. "I was finally going to beat you, fair and square. You knew you were going to lose, so you decided to sabotage the tournament."

Ava's eyes widened in surprise. "I would never do that!"

Ava's friends just stared at her. They all suspected her. They all thought she was guilty.

Tears stung her eyes. Ava ran from the training room.

23 ⁂

"Ava, wait!" Gabby ran after her.

Ava tried not to cry. "Do you think I'm guilty too?"

Gabby wrapped her sister in a tight hug. "Of course not!"

Ava sniffled. "But the others think I am!"

"Just because someone looks guilty doesn't mean they are. We need to clear your name. Which means we need to figure out what really made Sensei Suki sick."

"It's a mystery!" Erk croaked from Ava's pocket.

Ava smiled. She always felt better with her sister by her side. "A mystery only the ninja princess detectives can solve!" she said.

Chapter Three

A Dead End

Ava and Gabby reached in their backpacks. "Time to put on our thinking crowns!" they said together. With the golden crowns on their heads, they could crack any case.

Gabby pulled out her pink sparkly notebook and her fluffy unicorn pen. She opened the notebook to a new page. "We just need to follow the clues."

"Let's start at the beginning," Ava said. "If the brownie cookie made her sick, maybe one of the ingredients was tainted."

"Bad eggs?" Erk croaked.

Gabby scribbled down a list of ingredients. "We should visit Chef Pickles."

Ava and Gabby broke into a run, heading toward the royal kitchen on the other side of the palace.

"Rib-rib-ribbit!" Erk croaked unhappily as he bounced in Ava's pocket.

"Hold on, Erk!" Ava panted.

When they reached the kitchen, Chef Pickles was busy shoving freshly-made chicken finger pizzas into the large oven. He shut the oven door, turned around, and eyed Gabby's sparkly notebook. "Another mystery is afoot, I see."

They explained what happened. "Could the ingredients in the brownie cookie have accidentally made Sensei Suki sick?" Ava asked.

"Absolutely not!" Chef Pickles bellowed. "My kitchen is pristine! Every item is hand-picked from the best farms in Klue. I have only the highest standards!"

"Of course," Gabby said quickly. "But isn't there a chance—"

"Wait, did you say brownie cookie?" Chef Pickles asked.

The sisters nodded.

His cheeks turned red above his already-red beard. "I might have sampled a bit of the cookie dough when you weren't looking. It was delicious."

Ava perked up. "Do you feel sick at all?"

Chef Pickles straightened to his full height. "I've never felt better!"

"So it wasn't the cookie," Gabby said. "Or Chef Pickles would have gotten sick too."

"A dead end," Erk croaked.

Chef Pickles pointed them toward the door. "No frogs in my kitchen!"

"Yes, sir," Ava said.

"Wait, what's that?" Gabby pulled out her purple, jewel-covered magnifying glass. Right there on the steel counter was a smear of orange powder. "Another clue!"

"Mateo was eating cheese crackers!" Ava said. "He was here!"

Gabby nodded. "Maybe Mateo put something in the brownie cookie between the time Chef Pickles tasted it and when you picked it up."

"I did run to Klue Grocery for more frosting for my red velvet cupcakes," Chef Pickles said. "I mysteriously ran out."

"Hmm," Ava said.

"Mateo had the means and the opportunity," Gabby said.

"But what was his motive?" Ava asked. "He said he didn't care whether he won or lost the competition."

"We need to interview him to find out," Gabby said. "He's our prime suspect."

"The plot thickens!" Erk croaked.

Chapter Four

Explain Yourself!

"We know it was you," Gabby said as soon as they pulled Mateo out into the hallway. The rest of the class was still in the training room, talking, snacking, or practicing.

"I'm innocent," Mateo said.

"You still have orange cheese powder on your cheek!" Gabby said. "We found some on the counter next to the fridge where Ava stored the brownie cookie."

"Oh," Mateo said sheepishly.

"Confess," Ava said. "We promise we'll go easy on you."

"Okay, okay." Mateo held up his hands. "I was in the royal kitchen this morning."

"Aha!" Ava crowed.

"But it's not what it looks like."

Erk poked his head out of Ava's pocket and glared at Mateo with suspicious froggy eyes.

"Explain yourself!" Gabby said.

Mateo hung his head. "I snuck some marshmallow frosting from Chef Pickles's red velvet cupcakes. I really love that frosting."

Ava and Gabby exchanged glances. Mateo's story checked out. It matched up with Chef Pickles's missing frosting. They'd caught one thief—but not the right one.

"You're off the hook with us," Gabby said with a sigh. "But not with Chef Pickles."

"I know," Mateo said. "I'll go tell him after class."

Gabby scratched Mateo's name off the list of suspects. Now they were back to zero.

"It wasn't the brownie cookie after all," Ava said. "But what was it?"

Gabby tapped her thinking crown as she thought. "It has to be something Sensei Suki ate or drank. We need to interview the victim."

Five minutes later, Ava and Gabby stood outside one of the royal guest rooms where Sensei Suki was resting. She sat on a pink velvet sofa. Her purse was on the cushion next to her.

"How are you feeling?" Ava asked.

Sensei Suki pressed her hand to her

stomach. "I feel better now. It was worse this morning."

Gabby scribbled notes with her unicorn pen. "What else have you had to eat and drink today?"

"Only a few crackers, ginger ale, and water. I haven't been very hungry lately."

"Could it be the soda?" Ava asked.

Sensei Suki shook her head. "It was sealed when I opened it this morning."

"Hmm," Gabby said.

Sensei Suki frowned slightly as she picked up her purse and set it in her lap. "My purse is open. That's strange. I was sure it was closed."

"Have you had it with you the whole time?" Ava asked.

Sensei Suki nodded. "But I haven't used it since..."

"Since you put the brownie cookie inside," Gabby said. She closed her eyes, thinking back to that morning's events. She breathed in and out, focusing her mind the way the sensei had taught her. "Your purse was closed in the training room. I remember you zipped it."

Sensei Suki reached inside her purse and pulled out a package of saltine crackers. "This is odd."

"Those aren't your crackers?" Ava guessed.

"No." Sensei Suki opened them up and took a bite. "Someone must have put them there, somehow. Just like someone left a package of saltine crackers beside my ginger ale yesterday. And three days ago, I found another one on the hood of my car."

"It was Alex!" Ava whispered, using some ninja concentration powers of her own. "Your purse was zipped shut. Now it's not. The only person to touch your purse was Alex. When he tripped and fell, he slipped the crackers inside!"

"The crackers are making you sick!" Gabby said. "They're tainted!"

"The crackers are fine," Sensei Suki said.

"Alex is the culprit!" Ava cried.

"Yes, but it's not what you think," Sensei Suki said with a small smile. "Girls, you should know—"

"Wait!" Ava said. The pieces of the puzzle clicked together in her head. Sensei Suki's strange sickness. The ginger ale her husband kept bringing her. The fact that she wasn't hungry even for a delicious brownie cookie. How she kept touching her belly.

"We've cracked the case!" Ava shouted.

"Ribbit! The case is cracked," Erk croaked.

"We have? It is?" Gabby asked. Then her

eyes widened as she figured it out too. "We have! It is!"

"I do believe you figured it out," Sensei Suki said as she rose from the sofa. "Do you want to tell everyone together?"

Ava and Gabby grinned. "We sure do!"

Chapter Five

The Guilty One

O nce everyone was gathered back in the training room, Sensei Suki smiled at Alex. "It was you, Alex."

"It wasn't Ava after all?" Jade asked.

Mateo looked confused. "Alex is the guilty one?"

"It's not Alex making Sensei Suki sick," Ava said. "Or me."

Sensei Suki looked at the class. "Well, I was going to wait to tell anyone for a few more months, but we have some excellent detectives in this class."

Ava and Gabby curtsied playfully. Their friends laughed.

"Alex did smuggle crackers into my purse," Sensei Suki said. "But it was to help me."

"Help you what?" Jade asked.

"I haven't been feeling well, but I'm not sick. Not at all."

Ella's mouth dropped open. "You're not sick..."

"...but you have a sickness," Bella said.

"Now that's a mystery!" Daniella finished.

"It's a riddle, one we can finally solve," Ava said. "Sensei Suki is pregnant!"

The class gasped and squealed.

Sensei Suki put a finger to her lips.

"Can we keep it a surprise until after the tournament?"

"We sure can!" Ella said.

Bella jumped up and down. "Our lips are sealed!"

"Your secret is safe with us!" Daniella said.

"How did you know?" Gabby asked Alex. It wasn't often that a clue slipped by the ninja sisters. He'd figured it out first.

Alex gave an embarrassed shrug. "Ninja sense, remember? Plus, my mom just had my baby brother. Sensei Suki acted the same way my mom did. Sometimes pregnancy makes you feel sick for a while. Saltine crackers helped my mom. I wanted to help Sensei Suki too."

Sensei Suki smiled. "And you did! I feel much better. Thank you, Alex."

"Why didn't you say something when Mateo accused Ava?" Gabby asked.

Alex blushed. "I wanted to, but I didn't want to give away Sensei Suki's surprise. That's why I put the crackers in her purse in secret. I'm sorry."

"I understand," Ava said. "And I forgive you. Our job, after all, is to solve mysteries."

"Is the tournament still on?" Gabby asked hopefully.

Sensei Suki smiled. "Of course! It'll take a lot more than a little morning sickness to stop me! Now, who wants to help finish up the decorations?"

Chapter Six

Showers Ahead

The next day, everyone in Klue Kingdom came to watch the Taekwondo Tournament of Champions. Principal Knight, Miss Olsen, Mr. Harris, and Miss Fix-It all reserved front-row seats. Mom and Dad beamed down at the princesses from their thrones of honor.

"We're proud of your hard work," Dad said.

"Do your best," Mom said. "That's what matters."

Gabby showed off her breaking techniques. She broke three wooden boards in a row with just one hand. Ella, Bella, and Daniella performed perfect eagle strike and tiger claw movements.

When it was Ava's turn, she did an excellent set of flying kicks. Jade was next. Her spinning hook kicks and jumping axe kicks were flawless.

As Ava expected, Jade took top prize. Ava felt a little sad. She wanted to win, but Jade earned the prize, fair and square.

Second place wasn't so bad. Besides, there was always next year.

After the trophies were handed out, Sensei Suki gathered her entire class around her before she made her big announcement.

The whole kingdom burst into applause.

"Oh, baby shower planning!" Mr. Posh cried happily. "I can't wait!"

Sensei Suki leaned down and whispered to Ava and Gabby. "I'm glad I got to announce my pregnancy like this. Today is the best day ever. I think you two would make excellent babysitters. What do you say?"

Ava and Gabby grinned at each other. Ava's smile was so big, it was a mystery how it fit on her face.

NPD Academy

Ninja Basics

In ancient Japan, ninjas were expert warriors and spies. They were trained in martial arts from a young age. They learned to fight, but they preferred to use stealth.

Ninjas wore dark clothes so they could hide in the dark. They wore special socks instead of shoes to sneak around quietly. They also had metal claws they put on their feet to climb the walls of tall buildings.

Some people thought ninjas had magical powers. They believed ninjas could fly and even walk on water. While they weren't magical, ninjas were strong, skilled, patient, and smart problem-solvers!

Super Ninja Skills You Can Use

Invisibility

Ninjas aren't actually invisible, but they can hide in plain sight! Ninjas are known for their ability to remain completely still and blend in with their environment. Try it at home, but be careful not to scare anyone!

Flexibility

Ninjas use their flexibility to hide in tight spaces. Your flexibility can help keep your body fit! Bend over at the waist and reach toward your toes. Can you easily touch them? Try this every day for a week and see how your flexibility increases with practice.

Writing Mysteries

Mysteries are a genre, or category, of literature that focus on solving a mysterious problem, crime, or situation. A mystery has five basic elements:

1. **The mystery!** A pet goes missing. A favorite toy is stolen. Something strange happens, and no one knows why.

2. **The detective(s).** The detective is the character who investigates the situation, interviews witnesses, and eventually solves the case.

3. **Clues**. Clues are evidence that help lead the detective to the solution. And then there are red herrings! A red herring is a fake clue that authors put in a mystery to throw the detective (and the reader!) off the right track.

4. **The suspect(s).** Every good mystery has at least one suspect, or person the detective thinks is responsible. Two or three suspects makes it harder to solve the case. The detective must collect evidence to prove the suspect is guilty.

5. **The solution!** Solving the case is the best part of every mystery. The detective puts all the clues together and figures out the answer to the puzzle. The real clues need to make sense and help the detective crack the case.

Try It!

Ask a friend or family member to give you a person's name, an object, and a place. Now you have a character, a stolen object, and a setting! Write a mystery story based on these prompts.

Make Triple Chocolate Brownie Cookies

Ask an adult to help you make this story-inspired recipe!

Ingredients

- ¾ cup (170 grams) salted butter
- 4 ounces (113 grams) unsweetened chocolate, chopped
- 4 eggs
- 2 cups (454 grams) white sugar
- 1½ cups (339 grams) all-purpose flour
- ½ cup (113 grams) unsweetened cocoa powder
- 2 teaspoons (10 grams) baking powder
- ½ teaspoon (2 grams) salt
- ½ cup (113 grams) semisweet chocolate chips

Directions

1. In a microwave-safe bowl, heat chocolate and butter (30 seconds at a time) until the butter is melted. Stir until smooth.

2. In a larger bowl, beat eggs and sugar. Stir in the chocolate mixture.

3. Combine the flour, cocoa, baking powder, and salt in a separate bowl.

4. Slowly add the dry ingredients to the wet ingredients and mix well.

5. Mix in the chocolate chips.

6. Cover the bowl and chill in the refrigerator for two hours.

7. Preheat the oven to 350 degrees Fahrenheit (177 degrees Celsius).

8. For each cookie, scoop out two tablespoons (28 grams) of chilled dough and roll it into a ball. Place on a parchment-lined baking sheet and bake for seven to nine minutes. The tops of the cookies should begin to crack.

9. Remove the cookies from the oven.

10. Let the cookies cool on the baking sheet to for a few minutes before moving them to a cooling rack. Store in an airtight container at room temperature.

11. Enjoy!

About the Author

Kyla Steinkraus has been writing stories since she was five years old. Before she could write, she told stories into a recorder. Her parents still have some of them! Kyla lives with her two kids, her husband, and two very spoiled cats in Atlanta, Georgia. When she's not writing, Kyla loves hiking in the mountains, reading awesome books, and playing board games with her family. She has been known to jump out of a plane occasionally—parachute included, of course!

About the Illustrator

Katie Wood has loved drawing since she was very small, which inspired her to study illustration at Loughborough University. She now feels extremely lucky to be drawing every day from her studio in Leicester, England. She is never happier than when she is drawing with a cup of tea, or walking in the countryside with her unhelpful studio assistant, Inka the dog.